D1126572

APR

DEMCO

Short Vowel Phonics 5:
Catfish and Bass
and other tales

Compounds words, **kn,-nch,-nk,-tch,** and vowel y

by: Patricia J. Norton

illustrated by: Sarah E. Cashman
and Patricia J. Norton

About this book:

<u>Short Vowel Phonics 5</u> is the next book in the Short Vowel Phonics series after book 4. In this book the reader will experience short vowel words joined to make compound words and short vowel words containing kn, -nch, -nk, -tch, and vowel y.

On pages i and ii young readers can practice reading the compound words found in the stories.

non-phonetic sight words: a, as, has, his, is, of, the, they, to

Other reading material by the Author:
Short Vowel Phonics 1
Short Vowel Phonics 2 a, i
Short Vowel Phonics 2 o, u, e
Short Vowel Phonics 3
Short Vowel Phonics 4
Short Vowel Phonics Short Stories
Decodable Alphabet Chart

ISBN: 978-0-9817710-5-2 (lib. bdg.)
[1. Reading - Phonetic method. 2. Reading readiness. 3. Phonics]

shortvowelphonics.com

Printed and bound in Missouri, U.S.A.

Text font: Pen Time Manuscript

Table of Contents

Compound Word Practice

Catfish and Bass   page i
A Hen Hutch   page i
Drumming on a Drumset   page ii
Quilting at the Whitts   page ii

Chapter 1:   Mom Frost and Junk   Page 1

Phonetic concept: -unk words
Sight words: a, has, his, is, of, the, to
Vocabulary Preview: funk, "slam dunk"
word count: 112

Chapter 2:   Think Pink Sink!   Page 4

Phonetic concept: -ink words
Sight words: a, has, his, of, the
Vocabulary Preview: skink, mink
word count: 39

Chapter 3:   Catfish and Bass

Phonetic concept: compound words
Sight words: a, has, his, is, of, the, they, to

Part 1:   The Frosts Plan a Trip   Page 9

word count: 98

Part 2:   Camping   Page 12

Vocabulary Preview: bass, catfish, redbuds, sunfish
word count: 197

Part 3: **Fishing at Sunup**   **Page 17**
Vocabulary Preview: jig, jigging (as related to fishing)
word count: 88

Part 4: **Jigging with Jon**   **Page 19**
Vocabulary Preview: bluff (noun), flick
silent consonant: wr
word count: 109

Chapter 4: A Knock   Page 21
Phonetic concept: **kn** words
Sight words: a, has, is, the
Vocabulary Preview: knack, knit, weld
word count: 35

Chapter 5: A Hen Hutch   Page 23
Phonetic concept: -**tch**, compound, and -**ink** words
Sight words: a, has, his, is, of, the, they, to
Vocabulary Preview: clutch, hen hutch
        Lek is a Thai male name meaning "small"
word count: 168

Chap. 6: Drumming on a Desktop Page 27
Phonetic concept: compound, **kn**, and -**tch** words
Sight words: a, his, is, of, the, to
Vocabulary Preview: jazz band, rock band
word count: 151

Chapter 7: Lunch   Page 31
Phonetic concept: -**nch** and -**nk** words
Sight words: a, has, his, is, of, the, they, to
Vocabulary Preview: six-inch sub
word count: 125

Chapter 8: Quilting at the Whitts

Phonetic concept: compound words, -nch,-nk,-tch.
Sight words: a, has, his, is, of, they, to

Part 1: The Quilt Top   Page 35

Vocabulary Preview: jiff, patch (noun), sashing,
    scrap (noun), silk

word count: 192

Part 2: Quilting   Page 39

word count: 88

Part 3: The Quilt   Page 42

word count: 56

Chapter 9: In Sync   Page 44

Phonetic concept: vowel y, silent consonant -mn
Vocabulary Preview: lynx, "in sync"
Sight words: a
word count: 13

Notes to Parents and Teachers:

Catfish and Bass is inspired by a favorite Missouri pastime--
fishing. The story takes place at the Peabody Nature
Preserve, which is 4 miles west of Rich Hill, MO. The town
of Linn has several state conservation areas for fishing. One
type of fishing is called jigging. A jig is a hook with a heavy weight
attached to a line. Jigging is bobbing the jig up and down. The
Missouri Dept. of Conservation's staff helped insure the story's
accuracy.

A Hen Hutch tells the story of caring for hens. Chickens
come in many breeds. In the story is a "Dutch" hen. Dutch hens,
which contain many subgroups, were developed in the
Netherlands. The Blue Dutch Bantam chicken, with its red
comb and gray feathers, originated in Indonesia. Dutch
sailors brought the breed to the Netherlands centuries ago.

Catfish and Bass

cat fish	catfish	catfish
sun fish	sunfish	sunfish
red buds	redbuds	redbuds
set up	setup	setup
sun set	sunset	sunset
sun up	sunup	sunup
tip top	tiptop	tiptop
in to	into	into

The Hen Hutch

sun up	sunup	sunup
sun set	sunset	sunset

Drumming on a Desktop

desk top	desktop	desktop
lap top	laptop	laptop
pad lock	padlock	padlock
up hill	uphill	uphill
back up	backup	backup
with in	within	within
drum stick	drumstick	drumstick
drum set	drumset	drumset

Quilting at the Whitts

| in to | into | into |
| granddad | granddad | granddad |

Chapter 1

Mom Frost and Junk

It is spring. Mom's wish is to rid the Frost dwelling of mess. But Jon has a lot of junk. Mom tells Jon: "Get rid of this junk."

Jon is in a funk. Jon sits on his bunk. Then it 'sunk' in, "This spot is a mess." Jon has a plan. It's a "slam dunk" of a plan.

Jon gets a box and packs it.
Jon drags in a chest. Jon
stuffs it to the top. Then Jon
gets a trunk. Jon fills up the
trunk.

Jon quits and drops on his bunk. Not a spot of mess is left. Mom grins and hugs Jon.

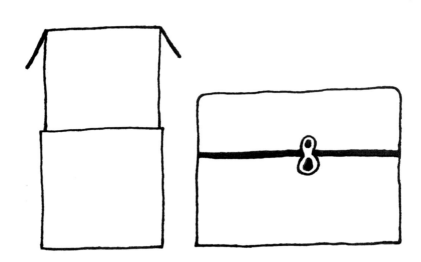

Think Pink Sink!

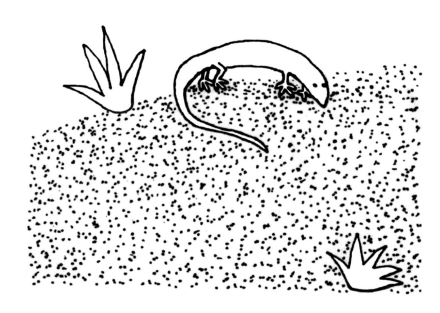

Can a skink get a drink in
the sands of Chad?

Can a mink wink at his mom

and dad?

Can a pink sink stink this bad?

The end of "Think Pink Sink!"

has us glad.

Chapter 3

Catfish and Bass

1. The Frosts Plan a Trip

Jon: "Fishing is fun. Let's plan a big fishing trip."

Mom: "Rich Hill has fishing ponds next to it. Lots of bass and sunfish swim in the ponds. And Rich Hill has an inn."

Tom: "Rich Hill it is! But at an inn?! Let's camp."

Mom: "Camp? In a tent?"

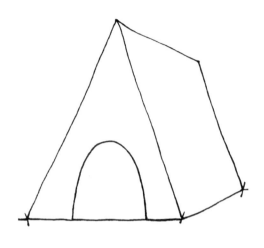

Tom and Jon yell, "YES!"

Mom: "But an inn has beds."

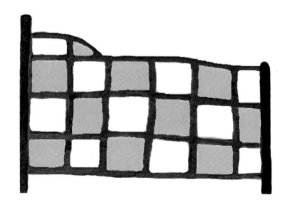

Jon: "But camping is fun, Mom."

Tom adds, "Camping is just west of Rich Hill. And it is next to the fishing ponds."

2. Camping

Mom gets a tent. The Frosts pack up the van. They trek to Rich Hill. They pass the inn. Mom's wish is to stop and check in. But Mom treks on.

Fishing Pond

CHECK INN

$49

They get to the camping spot. Which camping lot is best? Mom spots a lot next to a stand of redbuds. Tom spots a lot with a brick pit that they can grill on. Jon spots a lot next to a pond. They pick the lot with the brick pit. The camp setup is quick.

Next, Mom, Tom, and Jon fish. Jon gets a sunfish. Tom

gets a bass. And Mom gets

a sunfish. They let the fish

back into the pond.

Mom spots frogs hopping to

the pond. Tom spots frogs swimming in the pond. Jon spots frog eggs in the pond.

But at sunset the bugs get to Mom. Mom is not grinning. Mom packs the kids in the van. They trek to Rich Hill to sup. When they get back to camp, they step into the tent. Mom zips up the tent flap. The bugs still buzz.

The frogs sing: "Rib-it.........
Rib-it.........Rib-it."

Zap! The frogs sup on bugs.

3. Fishing at Sunup

At sunup, they got up and went to fish. With fishing rods and landing nets, Mom and Tom went fishing. They got catfish. With a rod and a jig, Jon went jigging. Jon got a bass.

Back at camp, Mom grills the fish. Mom, Jon, and Tom: "YUM."

Mom: "Fishing is fun. This is

a tiptop fishing trip."

Jon: "The next fishing trip is to Linn. Linn has lots of fishing spots."

Mom: "And Linn has an inn?"

4. Jigging with Jon

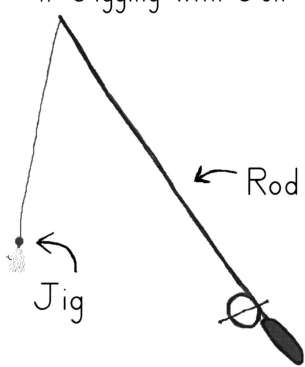

Rod

Jig

Jon went jigging. Jon had a jig on a rod. Jon sat on a rock next to the pond. Jon held the rod and let the jig drop into the pond. With a

19

flick of his wrist, the rod went up. Then, Jon let the rod drop a bit. The rod went up a bit. Jon let the rod drop. On and on it went. This is jigging.

Jon sits and jigs. The jig is up. The jig drops. A fish spots the jig. The fish thinks it is a bug. The fish gets the jig. The rod bends. Jon has a bass!

A Knock

Vic's rig went up a hill.

A hiss, a Knock, a CRACK.

And then, the rig went still.

In fixing things, Vic had

a knack.

A quick hot weld, did knit

the crack.

The Hen Hutch

Lek has a hen hutch in the back of his dwelling. In the hutch is a flock of hens. Lek tends to the hens. Lek tends them at sunup and sunset.

At sunup the hens get up and cluck. Lek gets up to fetch the hens' mash. Lek brings the mash to the hutch. Lek lifts the latch on the hutch.

23

The mash is fed to the hens.
The hens strut to the pen and
wish to drink. Lek fills the
drinking cans. The hens drink.

The hens scratch in the
grass. They dig in a ditch.
They snatch up bugs. The hens
fill up on bugs and grass.

At sunset the hens will nest
in the hutch. Lek will fill the
drinking cans. Then Lek will

latch up the hutch.

_ _ _ _ _

Lek has a Dutch hen. The hen has 3 eggs in a nest. The hen sits on the clutch of eggs till they hatch. When 21 sunsets pass, then the eggs will hatch.

Drumming on a Desktop

Ted sits at his desk drumming.

Knock, knock.

Ted's pals, Mitch and Nick, drop in.

Ted gets his laptop. Ted logs on and gets to the Web. Ted clicks on a list of bands.

Nick spots "Padlock," a jazz band. "Let's click on that band. The drumming is not bad."

27

Ted: "The sax is shrill. Let's skip it. Let's click on the rock band 'Uphill.' It's the backup band to 'Within.' The drumming is tops."

Nick and Mitch pick the rock band. Ted clicks on "Uphill." Nick hums with the band. Mitch claps. Ted drums with his drumsticks. When the band stops, Ted is still drumming on his desktop.

Mitch: "Ted, the desktop will get dents with that drumming. Get a drumset."

Nick adds, "And get a set of

plugs--a gift to a mom and a dad."

Ted grins.

Lunch

Sid and Jim sat in math class. They had math class with Miss Finch. The class had a bunch of sums to add. Jim and Sid had lots of sums to add up.

Miss Finch: "Class, it's 12:00. Hand in the math sums."

The class went to lunch. Sid and Jim got lunch. Sid's lunch had fish and chips, milk, and a plum. Jim's lunch had a six-inch sub, milk, and a plum. They went and sat on the bench next to the swing sets. They had lunch. Munch, munch.

Jim sniffs. Sid sniffs. They

sniff a stench. A skunk is next
to the swing sets. Jim drops
his lunch and runs. Sid drops
his lunch and runs. The skunk
will crunch on a big lunch.

33

Chapter 8

Quilting at the Whitts

1. The Quilt Top

Meg Whitt has a wish list. On Meg's list is "a 9-patch scrap quilt." Mom plans to stitch Meg a quilt.

Mom must get lots of scraps with which to quilt. Mom has a stash of scraps. Meg digs into Mom's stash. In a jiff, Meg picks a big stack of scraps.

Dad tells the Whitt clan,

"Mom will stitch a scrap quilt.

It is a gift to Meg."

Dad's kin send scraps to

Mom. Dad's sis, Bev, sends

scraps. Beth Ann has a red and black dress. Seth has a tan vest. Bev sends scraps of the dress and vest. Granddad has a pink silk dress of his mom. Granddad sends a cut of pink silk. Mom gets lots of scraps with which to stitch the quilt.

Mom plans the quilt top. Mom and Dad cut the scraps into six-inch blocks. Mom and

Meg stitch the blocks into 9-patch blocks. Dad cuts the sashing strips. Mom and Meg stitch the sashing to the 9-patch blocks. At last, Mom has a big quilt top.

sashing

9-patch block

2. Quilting

Mom sets in the quilt. To "set in the quilt," Mom has to pin and stretch the backing. Then, on top of the backing is the batting. On top of the batting is the quilt top.

Mom pins the quilt top to
the backing. The pinning ends.

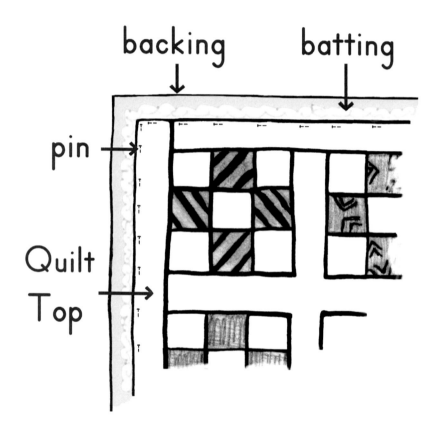

backing   batting

pin →

Quilt
Top →

Mom can quilt the quilt.
A lot of quilting is in a quilt.

Mom quilts and quilts. Mom thinks quilting is fun. At last, the quilting is at an end. Meg has a scrap quilt. Mom is glad.

3. The Quilt

Meg held the quilt. Meg felt the blocks of Beth Ann and Seth. Meg felt the pink silk blocks.

"Is the pink silk a scrap of a wedding dress?" Meg asks.

Dad: "Granddad can tell if it is. Ask him."

The quilt is on the bed. Meg grins and hugs Mom and Dad.

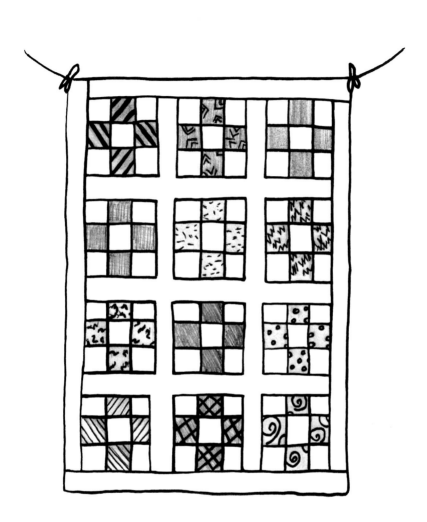

43

Chapter 9

<u>In Sync</u>

Miss Lynn and Miss Lynx

will sing a hymn

in sync.